VIKING

Published by Penguin Group

Penguin Group (USA), Inc., 345 Hudson Street, New York, New York 10014, U.S.A.

Penguin Books Ltd, 80 Strand, London WC2R 0RL, England

Penguin Books Australia Ltd, 250 Camberwell Road, Camberwell, Victoria 3124, Australia

Penguin Books Canada Ltd, 10 Alcorn Avenue, Toronto, Ontario, Canada M4V 3B2

Penguin Books (N.Z.) Ltd, 182-190 Wairau Road, Auckland 10, New Zealand

First published in 2003 by Viking, a division of Penguin Young Readers Group.

10 9 8 7 6 5 4 3 2 1

LIBRARY OF CONGRESS CATALOGING-IN-PUBLICATION DATA

Smith, Lane.

The happy Hocky family moves to the country! / by Lane Smith. p. cm.

Summary: When the Hocky family moves to a big old house in the country,
it takes them some time to adjust to a new way of life.

ISBN 0-670-03594-7

[1. Country life—Fiction. 2. Family life—Fiction. 3. Humorous stories.] I. Title.

PZ7.S6538Haq 2003

[E]—dc21

2002152206

Manufactured in China   Set in Janson.

Design: Molly Leach

The Happy Hocky Family moves to the Country

!

LANE SMITH

VIKING

To all the Enlows
and
To brother Shane

We Are the Hocky Family

I am Mr. Hocky!

I am Mrs. Hocky!

I am Baby Hocky!

I am Henry Hocky!

I am Holly Hocky!

I am Newton!

Country Home

See the big yellow truck?

The Hocky family is moving
from the CITY to the COUNTRY.
"How exciting!" say the Hockys.

Here is the Hocky family's new house.
Their new house is actually a very
OLD house.

It is a FUN house.
When it rains outside,
it rains inside, too.
Ha ha. What a FUN house.

City Words/Country Words

The
   city
    and
     the
      country
       have
        the
         same
          words
          but
           sometimes
           those
           words
           have
           different
            meanings . . .

City Words

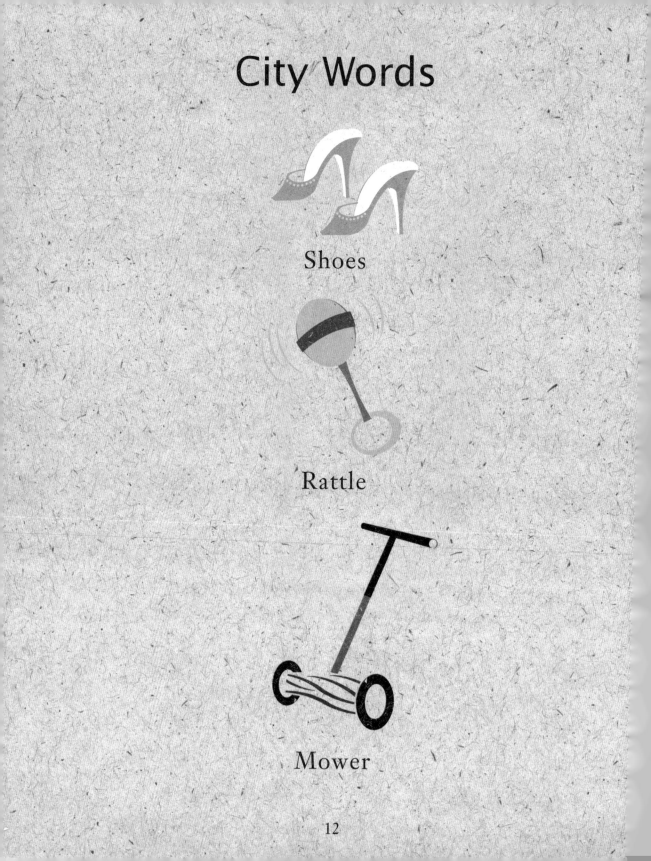

Shoes

Rattle

Mower

Country Words

Shoes

Rattle

Mower

City Words

Garbage collector

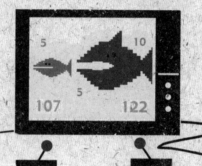

Toy

Milk

Country Words

Garbage collector

Toy

Milk

Country Time

In the city you use an alarm clock to wake up.

In the country you don't need one.

COCK-A-DOODLE-DOO

goes the neighbor's rooster at 5:30 in the morning.

Meet the Neighbor

Next door to the Hocky family lives
FARMER DILL.
Farmer Dill has LOTS of animals.

"LOOK," says Holly. "Chickens!"

"LOOK," says Henry. "Goats!"

"LOOK," says Mr. Hocky. "Geese!"

"LOOK," says Mrs. Hocky. "Cows!"

"LOOK," says Baby Hocky. "Pigs!"

SEE the wind CHANGE.

It was going THAT way.

Now it is going THIS way.

"PEE-YEW," says Holly. "CHICKENS!"
"YUCK," says Henry. "GOATS!"
"UGH," says Mr. Hocky. "GEESE!"
"WHOA," says Mrs. Hocky. "COWS!"
"WAAAH!" says Baby Hocky. "PIGS!"

Henry's Feeder

Look, Henry is filling his
BIRD FEEDER.

He is filling it with a special mix of
sunflower seeds for WOODPECKERS.

and cracked corn for CARDINALS

and peanut kernels for CHICKADEES.

"LISTEN.

Can you hear them?

They are coming already."

Poison Ivy/Poison Oak

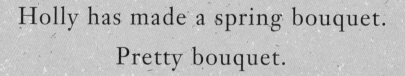

Holly has made a spring bouquet.

Pretty bouquet.

Uh oh.

ITCHY bouquet.

"Ha ha!" laughs Henry. "You used
POISON IVY.
Poison ivy has three leaves.
Can't you count to three? It's easy:
1, 2, 3.

"I am MUCH smarter.
I have used OAK leaves for mine."

County Fair

LIVESTOCK

PRODUCE

Do you know what a blue ribbon means?

It means FIRST PRIZE.

This is what Henry hopes

to win with the tomato he grew.

Masie P.

F. Dill Jr.

E. Delmer

LOOK!
The other boys and girls have
grown fruits and vegetables, too.

Do you know that Henry doesn't like
the color blue that much anyway?

Baby's Caterpillar Story

I have a caterpillar.
Do you have a caterpillar?
I have a caterpillar.

My caterpillar is fuzzy.

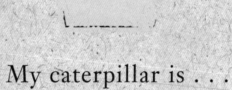

My caterpillar is . . .

?

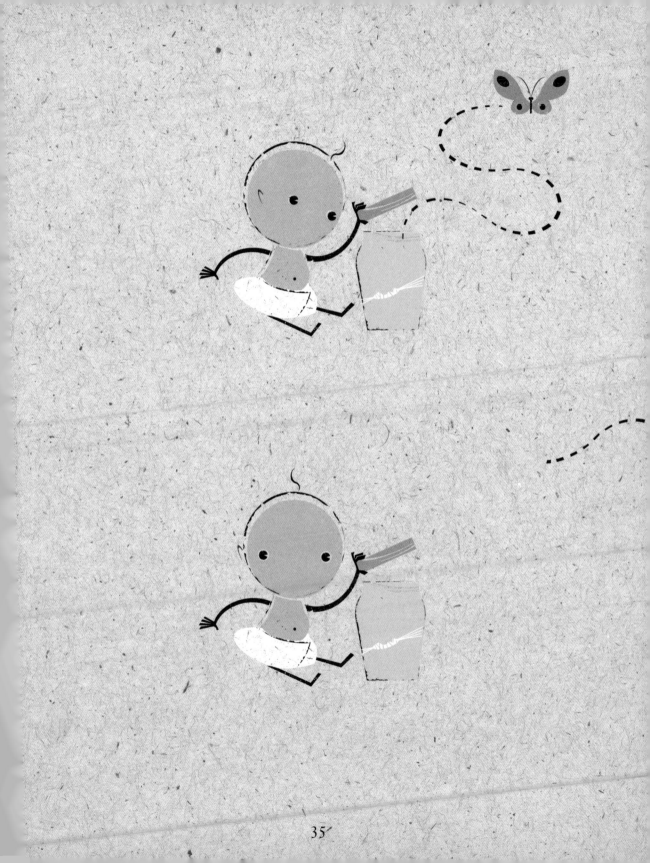

I have a jar.

Do you have a jar?

I have a jar.

Activities

TOWN CALENDAR

S	M	T	W	T	F	S
CHILI DINNER			CHILI DINNER			CHILI DINNER
	CHILI DINNER		CHILI DINNER			
		CHILI DINNER		CHILI DINNER		CHILI DINNER
	CHILI DINNER				BINGO	
	CHILI DINNER					

There is A LOT to do in
the Hockys' town of Old Newbury.

LOOK!

From all of the chili-dinner fund-raisers,
the town has made enough
money to build a new
SCHOOL CAFETERIA.

Let's go inside.

A + B = C
(Country Math)

A.

Here is the
wild bunny.

B.

Here is the wild
bunny's BIG belly.

turnips

carrots

carr

C.

Here is where Mrs. Hocky's
GARDEN used to be.

Henry's Bird Feeder (PART TWO)

Henry is fixing his bird feeder.
It is a lot of work, but it is worth
it to have the squirrel problem SOLVED.

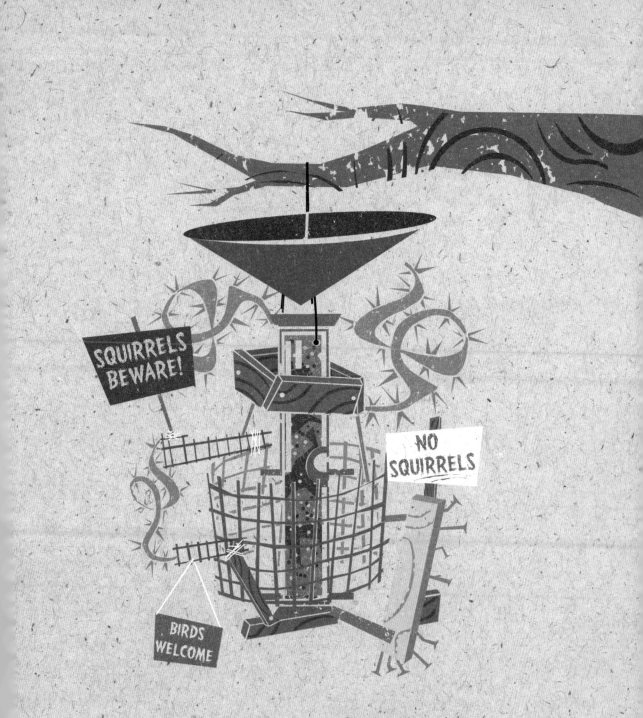

Listen, here come the birds!

Leaf Story

Leaves are a part of
NATURE.

Nature is GOOD.

But leaves must be RAKED.

Rake, Holly, rake.

Leaves are a part of

NATURE.

Nature is GOOD.

Baby's Friend

Baby Hocky has asked for an
extra dessert for his "friend."

He says his friend is fuzzy.
He says his friend is HUNGRY.

Mr. and Mrs. Hocky laugh at Baby's story.

He tells good stories.

This is called having an

IMAGINATION.

Here is Baby with his imaginary friend now.
LOOK at Mr. and Mrs. Hocky run for Baby.
RUN, Mr. and Mrs. Hocky, RUN!

Winter Game

In the country there are lots
of new games to play.
This one is called
FIND THE DRIVEWAY.

Snowman and Friend

Holly is showing Newton
how to make a snowman.
But Newton is cold.
Newton is BORED.

Later, Holly sees the
SNOW REINDEER Newton has made.
"What a trickster!" says Holly.
"You weren't really bored.
You were watching all along weren't you?
Weren't you Newton? Newton . . . ?"

Counting Game

If Farmer Dill's rooster
crows 17 times a day,
and the Hocky family
has heard him 6,205 times,
how long has the Hocky
family been in the country

?

You're right.

ONE

WHOLE

YEAR.

County Fair

(ONE YEAR LATER)

CRAFTS
FOR
SALE

HOLLY'S
LEAF WREATHS
$3.50 each

It is time again for the county fair.
LOOK! Holly has made eighty-
seven dollars and fifty cents
with her Leaf Wreaths™.

LOOK!

Mrs. Hocky has won a

RED RIBBON in the livestock contest!

LOOK!

Henry has won a

BLUE RIBBON in the arts and crafts contest!

LOOK!

Mr. Hocky is leading the parade!

The

Hocky

family

is

going

to

be

OKAY

in

the

country

!

Bedtime

"Good night Holly," says Henry.

"Good night Dad," says Holly.

"Good night Henry," says Mr. Hocky.

"Good night Baby," says Mrs. Hocky.

"Good night Newton," says Baby.

Cock-a-doodle-doo! Cock-a-doodle-doo!"

GOOD NIGHT ROOSTER!"

says the Hocky family.